# The Secret Garden

Adapted for the LeapPad by Sarah Verney

# Table of Contents

 I. Across the Moor

"I suppose I should tell you about where you are going," Mrs. Medlock said. "Do you know anything about your uncle?"

"No," said Mary Lennox. She looked up from her corner of the railway **carriage**. She did not like Mrs. Medlock. She seldom liked anyone.

"Didn't your father and mother talk about him?"

"No," said Mary. She frowned. Her mother and father had never told her much about anything. Her father had always been busy with his work. And her mother had had no interest in taking care of her. She had hardly seemed to belong to her parents at all.

"Humph," muttered Mrs. Medlock. She supposed

she should feel sorry for the child. After all, her parents had just died of **cholera**, a terrible disease. There had been an **epidemic** in **India**, where Mary had lived. She had lost nearly everyone she had known.

The only person Mary had left in the world was her uncle, Archibald Craven. It was Mr. Craven who had sent Mrs. Medlock to meet Mary after her long **voyage** to England. Mrs. Medlock was to bring her to **Misselthwaite Manor**, Mr. Craven's home in **Yorkshire**, England.

Mrs. Medlock had quickly discovered that Mary had been quite spoiled. In fact, she didn't feel sorry for her in the least. She was such a rude, unpleasant child!

"Well, I suppose you might as well be told something," Mrs. Medlock said finally. "You are going to a strange place."

Mary said nothing at all. She did not want Mrs. Medlock to think she was interested.

Mrs. Medlock went on, "It's a grand place, in a gloomy way. The house is six hundred years old. It's on the edge of the moor. There's near a hundred rooms in it, though most of them's shut up. And there's a big park round it and gardens and trees." She paused and took another breath. "But there's nothing else."

There was a short silence. "Well," Mrs. Medlock said. "What do you think of it?"

"Nothing," Mary answered. "I know nothing of such places."

"I don't know why you're to stay at Misselthwaite Manor, really," said Mrs. Medlock. Perhaps it's the easiest way." She stopped as if she had just remembered something. "He's got a crooked back," she added. "That set him wrong. Though he had a wife, you know."

Mary looked at Mrs. Medlock in surprise. She knew her uncle was a **hunchback**. But she hadn't known he was married.

"She was a sweet, pretty thing," Mrs. Medlock went on. "He'd have walked the world over to get her a blade of grass she wanted. And when she died–"

Mary started. "Oh! Did she die?" she **exclaimed**. She was surprised to find she suddenly felt sorry for Mr. Archibald Craven. She was not used to thinking of anyone but herself.

"Yes, she died," Mrs. Medlock said. "And it made him **odder** than ever. Now he cares about nobody. Most of the time he stays away, traveling. When he is at Misselthwaite he shuts himself up in the west wing. He won't let anyone see him."

Mary stared out the window. A house with a hundred rooms and a man with a crooked back who shut himself up! It was like something in a book!

"Don't expect to see him," said Mrs. Medlock. "And you're not to go wandering and poking about. Mr. Craven won't have it."

"I shall not want to poke about," said Mary, turning toward the window. Perhaps she did not feel sorry for her uncle after all. Perhaps he deserved all that had happened to him.

Soon Mary found herself seated in the corner of a horse-drawn carriage. "What is a **moor**?" she asked Mrs. Medlock.

"Look out of the window in about ten minutes and you'll see," Mrs. Medlock answered.

Mary waited as they drove through a tiny village. After that, she could see nothing but a dense darkness on either side. She leaned forward and pressed her face against the window. Just then, the carriage gave a big jolt.

"Eh! We're on the moor now," said Mrs. Medlock. The carriage lamps shed a yellow light on a rough road. It seemed to be cut through bushes and low-growing things that ended in a great expanse of dark. The wind made a low, rushing sound. Mary felt as though the **bleak** moor was an ocean through which she was passing on a strip of land.

"I don't like it," Mary said to herself.

At last they drew up by a long, low house that rambled round a stone court. An old man opened the door. "Take her to her room," he told Mrs. Medlock. "Mr. Craven doesn't want to see her. He's leaving in the morning."

Mary was led up a broad staircase and then down one long **corridor** after another. Finally she found herself in a room with a fire in it and a supper on a table.

"Well, here you are!" Mrs. Medlock said. "This room and the next are yours. You must keep to them. Don't you forget that!"

And so it was that Mary arrived at Misselthwaite Manor.

 II. Martha and Ben

Mary opened her eyes in the morning to find a young **housemaid** kneeling by the fire.

"What is that?" Mary asked, pointing out the window.

Martha grinned. "That's the moor. Does **tha'** like it?"

"No, I hate it" answered Mary. "You like it?"

"**Aye**, that I do," Martha answered, cheerfully polishing away. "I just love it. And so will you. It's fair lovely in the spring and summertime."

Mary listened to her and asked, "Are you going to be my servant?"

"I'm Mrs. Medlock's servant," Martha said **stoutly**. "But I'm to do the housemaid's work up here. And wait on you a bit."

"Then who is going to dress me?" demanded Mary.

Martha stared at her. "Cannot tha' dress **thy** self?"

"No," answered Mary **indignantly**. "I never did in my life. My **ayah** dressed me, of course." Mary's "ayah" had done most everything for her, in fact.

"It's time tha' should learn then," Martha said. After Mary had finished her breakfast Martha said, "You wrap up warm and run out and play now."

Mary went to the window. It was dull and **wintry** outside. "Out? Why should I go out on a day like this?" she said. Mary glanced about her. There was nothing to do. Perhaps it would be better to go out after all.

"If tha' goes round that way tha'll come to the gardens," said Martha. "There's lots of flowers in summer, but nothing's blooming now." Martha pointed to a gate, "One of them is locked up. No one has been in it for ten years."

"Why?" Mary asked.

"Mr. Craven had it shut up when his wife

died. He locked the door and **buried** the key. Oh! There's the bell—I must run."

As Mary walked outside she wondered about the garden. What did it look like? Was everything dead inside? She wandered down one path after another. Finally she came to a garden with ivy-covered walls all round it. Beyond it were several more walled gardens.

Mary stared. The place was bare and ugly.

Before long an old man walked through a door leading from one of the gardens.

"What is this place?" Mary asked rudely.

"One of the kitchen-gardens," the man answered shortly. He turned away. **Obviously**, he did not care to talk to her.

Mary followed the path from one garden to another. But there was one she could not get into. There were walls all round it, but there was no door.

Above the wall, Mary could see the tops of trees and a bird with a bright red breast. Suddenly he burst into a song so cheerful that it almost brought a smile to her **sour** little face. "Perhaps he knows all about the secret garden," she thought.

Mary walked back into the first kitchen-garden and found the old man again. He took no notice of her.

"I have been into the other gardens," Mary said. "A bird with a red breast was sitting on one of the **treetops**. He sang."

To her surprise, a slow smile spread over the **surly** face. The old gardener whistled softly. There was a rush of wings, and then the bird lit on a **clod** of earth near the gardener's foot.

"Where has tha' been, tha' **cheeky** little **beggar**?" the old man said to the bird.

The bird looked up, his head to one side, not the least bit afraid. He hopped about and pecked the earth briskly.

Mary got a strange feeling in her heart. He was so pretty and cheerful! "Will he always come when you call him?"

"Aye, that he will," the man said. "I've knowed him since he was a **fledgling**."

"What kind of a bird is he?" Mary asked.

"He's a **robin redbreast**. They're the friendliest birds alive. Watch him looking round at us now and again. He knows we're talking about him. He likes that, he does."

Now and then the bird stopped pecking and looked at them with great curiosity. The funny feeling in Mary's heart grew. "Where did the rest of his **brood** fly to?" she asked.

"There's no knowing, but this one knew he was lonely. So he stayed with me."

Mary went a step nearer to the robin and looked at him very hard. "I'm lonely," she said. She had not known it before, but this was one of the things that made her feel cross and sour.

The old gardener stared at her. "**Art** tha' the little **wench** from India?" he asked.

Mary nodded.

"Then no wonder tha' art lonely." He began to dig again.

"What is your name?" Mary inquired.

"Ben Weatherstaff. I'm lonely myself." He jerked his thumb toward the robin. "He's the only friend I've got."

"I have no friends at all," said Mary. "I never had. My ayah didn't like me. And I never played with anyone."

Suddenly a rippling sound broke out near her. The robin had flown to an apple tree and burst into song.

Ben Weatherstaff laughed. "He's made up his mind to make friends with thee."

"With me?" said Mary. She moved toward the little tree and looked up. "Would you make friends with me?" she said softly.

The robin gave a little shake of his wings, then flew away.

"He has flown over the wall!" Mary cried out, watching him. "He has flown into the garden where there is no door!"

"He lives there," said old Ben. "He's probably **courting** some young robin that lives in one of the rose-trees."

"Rose-trees," Mary said. "I should so like to see them. There must be a door."

Ben drove his spade deep. He looked as unfriendly as he had at first. "There was ten years ago, but there isn't now."

"No door!" cried Mary. "But there must be."

"None as anyone can find. Don't you poke your nose where it's no cause to go. Here, I must go on with my work. Now get you gone." And without another word, he threw his **spade** over his shoulder and walked off.

 III. The Cry in the Corridor

At first each day was just like the others. Mary wandered round the gardens and down the paths. Most often, she went to the long walk outside the gardens with the walls round them.

One day Mary noticed something strange about the wall on the long walk. On one part, the creeping dark leaves were more bushy than anywhere else. As she stood wondering why, she heard a brilliant **chirp**. There, on the top of the wall, perched Ben's robin.

"Oh!" she cried out. "Is it you? Is it you?"

The robin hopped along, twittering as if he were talking to her. Mary followed him, laughing. She chirped at him and tried to whistle. The robin chirped and whistled back at her. At last he darted to the top of a tree.

"He must be in the secret garden," Mary said. She looked closely at the ivy-covered wall. But it was just as before–there was no door in it. "It's very strange," she said. "There must have been one ten years ago, because Mr. Craven buried the key."

After supper that night, Mary sat on the hearth-rug with Martha. She liked hearing about Martha's eleven brothers and sisters, who lived with their parents in a small cottage on the other side of the moor. She especially liked hearing about Martha's brother Dickon, who could **charm** the wild creatures on the moor. When Mary needed to know something about her strange new home, she asked Martha. "Why did Mr. Craven hate the garden?" she asked now.

"Because it was Mrs. Craven's garden," Martha said. "She just loved it. But one day, she was sitting on a branch of an old tree, and it broke. She fell on the ground. And she was hurt so bad that the next day she died. That's why he hates it."

Mary stared at the fire and thought about poor Mr. Craven and his young wife. As Mary thought, she listened to the sound the wind made. It seemed louder than usual. Or was it...was it something else?

Mary looked at Martha. "Do you hear anyone crying?"

"Oh, no!" Martha looked alarmed. "That's just the wind."

"But listen," said Mary. "It's in the house, not outside..." Suddenly the door to Mary's room blew open with a crash. The crying sound swept down the corridor, clearer than ever.

"I told you so!" said Mary. "It is someone crying!"

Martha jumped up and closed the door. "It was the wind," said Martha stubbornly.

But something made Mary believe Martha was not speaking the truth.

The next day the rain came down in **torrents**, and Mary decided to explore the old house.

Mary wandered upstairs and down. She opened one door after another. All of the rooms were full of heavy, dark furniture and old pictures and **tapestries**.

At last Mary decided to turn back. But

before long she realized she was lost. She stood still a moment, thinking.

Suddenly a short, **fretful** cry broke the stillness. Mary's heart beat faster. "It is crying," she said. As she stood still, listening, she accidentally put her hand on the tapestry near her. Suddenly she sprang back. The tapestry covered a door! It fell open, showing her another corridor behind it.

Mary gasped. Mrs. Medlock was coming up the corridor!

"What are you doing here?" Mrs. Medlock said **crossly**. She took Mary by the arm. "What did I tell you?"

"I turned round the wrong corner," explained Mary. "I didn't know which way to go. I heard someone crying."

"You didn't hear anything of the sort," Mrs. Medlock said. She half-pushed, half-pulled Mary back to her own room.

Mary sat on the hearth-rug, pale with rage. She ground her teeth. "There was someone crying!" she said to herself. "There was—I know there was!"

 ## IV. Into the Garden

Two days later Mary awoke to a brilliant, deep blue sky. It was Martha's day off. She gave Mary breakfast, then took off over the moor to spend the day at her family's cottage.

Mary felt lonelier than ever when Martha left. How she wished she could go with Martha! She would love to meet her brothers and sisters, and especially Dickon.

Mary wandered out into the kitchen-garden, where she found Ben Weatherstaff. The change in the weather seemed to make him friendly again. "Springtime's coming," he said. "In the flower gardens you'll soon see green spikes sticking out of the black earth."

"What will they be?" asked Mary.

"**Crocuses** and **snowdrops** and **daffy-down-dillys**. They'll poke up a bit here and there. You watch them."

"I am going to," Mary said. Soon she heard the soft rustling of wings, and then the robin landed close to her feet.

"Are things stirring down in the dark in that garden where he lives?" Mary asked.

"What garden?" grunted Ben, becoming surly again.

"The one where the old **rose-trees** are," Mary said.

"Ask him," Ben said, nodding toward the robin. "He's the only one as has seen inside it for ten years." He turned away.

Mary walked away, thinking about the garden. She had begun to like the garden. She had begun to like the robin and Martha, too. She had even begun to like Dickon, though she hadn't met him. That was a good many things to like, when you were not used to liking.

Mary walked along the ivy-covered wall. The robin hopped next to her. She bent down, trying to make robin sounds. Just then, the robin hopped over a pile of freshly turned up earth.

There was something half buried in the newly-turned soil.

It was an old key! Mary picked it up, feeling almost frightened. "Perhaps it is the key to the garden!" she whispered.

What happened next seemed almost like Magic. Suddenly a gust of wind blew aside some of the loose ivy trails. Mary leapt forward, catching them in her hand. She had seen something—the knob of a door! With shaking hands, Mary found the lock below the knob. She put in the key and turned as hard as she could. The lock sprung open.

Mary looked quickly round, then pushed open the door. She was inside the secret garden!

It was the sweetest, most **mysterious**-looking place ever. Leafless stems of climbing roses covered the high walls. More climbing roses had run all over the trees and swung down long **tendrils**. Mary did not know whether they were dead or alive, but the thin brown branches spreading over everything made it look strange and **enchanting**.

As Mary walked round, she came upon some sharp, pale-green points sticking out of the dark earth. She knelt down to look at them. Maybe they were crocuses or snowdrops!

Mary searched the garden and found many more pale-green points. "It isn't a dead garden," she cried out softly. "Even if the roses are dead, there are other things alive."

But Mary was sure the green points did not have enough room to grow. She found a sharp piece of wood, then weeded until she made clear places all around them.

Mary enjoyed her work so much that she came to the garden every day for the next week.

One day, Mary even dared to ask Martha if she might have some tools and seeds to make a small garden of her own somewhere in the kitchen-gardens. Together they sent a letter to Martha's brother Dickon. He would buy the things for Mary, and then bring them to her himself, Martha promised.

Several days later, Mary was walking toward the secret garden when she heard a low whistle. Looking round, she saw a boy playing a wooden pipe. Nearby, a brown squirrel and two rabbits sat listening.

The boy had to be Dickon, Mary knew. Who else could charm the wild creatures like that?

The boy stood slowly, so as not to frighten the animals. "I'm Dickon," he said. "I know tha' art Miss Mary. I've brought the garden tools, and the seeds, too."

They sat down on a log together and looked at the seeds. Dickon told her how to care for them. "I'll plant them for **thee** myself," he said suddenly. "Where is tha' garden?"

Mary's thin hands clutched each other. Her face went red. She couldn't tell Dickon about the secret garden!

Mary held her hands tighter. "Could you keep a secret? I don't know what I should do if anyone found it out."

Dickon looked more puzzled. "Aye, I can keep secrets," he said.

"I've **stolen** a garden," Mary blurted out. "It isn't mine. It isn't anybody's. Nobody wants it but me."

"Where is it?" Dickon asked, his voice low.

Mary got up from the log. "I'll show you," she said.

She led him round to the door and pushed it slowly open. They walked in together. Dickon looked round and round. "I never thought I'd see this place," he added.

"Did you know about it?" Mary asked.

Dickon nodded. "Martha told me. Us used to wonder what it was like."

Mary put her hand on his arm. "Is it all dead?" she whispered.

"Eh! No! It's not all dead!" Dickon stepped over to the nearest tree. He took a knife out of his pocket. Opening the blade, he cut through a dry-looking branch. "There's green in that wood yet," he said happily. "If it's took care of there'll be a fountain of roses here this summer."

"Oh, Dickon," Mary cried. "Will you help me take care of it?"

"I'll come every day if tha' wants me," he answered.

Mary smiled at him. "Dickon, I like you," she said. "And you make the fourth person. I never thought I should like four people."

"Only four folk as tha' likes?" Dickon laughed. "Who is the other three?"

"Martha and Ben Weatherstaff." Mary checked

them off on her fingers. "And the robin, too."

Dickon laughed. "I know tha' thinks I'm a strange **lad**," he said. "But I think tha' art the strangest little lass I ever saw."

Mary leaned forward. "Do you like me?" she said. She had never even dreamed of asking such a question before.

"Eh! That I does," Dickon answered. "I likes thee wonderful. And so does your robin, I do believe!"

"That's two, then," said Mary. She clapped her hands. "That's two for me."

Mary was sorry when the big clock struck the hour of her **midday** dinner. She slowly walked to the door. Then she stopped and walked back. "Whatever happens, you...you never would tell?" she said.

Dickon smiled. "If tha' was a **missel thrush** and showed me where thy nest was, does tha' think I'd tell? Not me," he said. "Tha' art as safe as a missel thrush."

And she was quite sure she was.

 V. "I Am Colin"

Mary woke that night to the sound of a howling wind and fierce rain beating against her window. There would be no working in the garden tomorrow, she realized. She lay in bed, angry and **miserable**.

After about an hour, Mary suddenly sat up. She turned toward the door, listening. "That isn't the wind," she said to herself. She got out of bed, picking up the candle on her table, and walked softly out of her room.

Mary followed the sound of the crying all the way to the tapestry door. She went through, closing the door behind her. A bit farther on she went through another door, into a room filled with ancient, handsome furniture. Against the wall was a four-posted bed. And in it was a boy, crying **fretfully**.

Mary crept across the room. The boy turned and stared at her. His face was **delicate** and pale, as though he had been ill.

"Who are you?" he whispered. "Are you a ghost?"

"No," Mary answered. "Are you?"

The boy stared. What strange eyes he had, Mary thought. They had thick black lashes and looked too big for his face.

"No," the boy replied after a moment. "I am Colin Craven. Mr. Craven is my father."

"Your father!" gasped Mary. "No one ever told me he had a boy! Mr. Craven is my uncle. I am Mary Lennox."

"Come here," Colin demanded. Mary came close to the bed. He reached out to touch her. "Where did you come from?"

"From my room. Did no one ever tell you about me?"

"No," Colin answered. "They dare not."

"Why?" asked Mary.

"Because I should have been afraid you would see me. I won't let people see me and talk about me. I won't."

"Why?" Mary asked again.

"Because I am always ill. If I live I may be a hunchback. But I won't live. My father won't let people talk about me, either. He hates to think I may be like him."

"Does he come and see you?" Mary asked.

"Sometimes. When I am asleep. He doesn't want to."

"Why?" Mary could not help asking again.

A shadow passed over the boy's face. "My mother died when I was born. It makes him sad to look at me. He thinks I don't know, but I've heard people talking. He almost hates me."

"He hates the garden, because she died," Mary said.

"What garden?" the boy asked.

"Oh! Just—just a garden she used to like," Mary **stammered**. Too late, she realized she should not have mentioned it. "Have you been here always?" she asked.

"Nearly always. Sometimes I have been taken to places at the seaside. But I won't stay because people stare at me. A grand doctor came from **London** to see me. He said they should keep me out in the fresh air. But I hate fresh air!"

"If you don't like people to see you, do you want me to go away?" Mary asked.

"No," he said. "Stay and talk. I want to hear about you."

Mary put her candle on the table and sat on a **footstool**. She told Colin all about India and her voyage across the ocean. She learned about Colin, too. He could have anything he asked for and was never made to do anything he didn't like to do.

"How old are you?" Colin asked at one point.

"I am ten," answered Mary. Forgetting herself for the moment, she went on. "And so are you."

"How do you know that?" he demanded, surprised.

Mary bit her lip. "Because when you were born the garden was locked up. And it has been locked for ten years."

Colin half sat up. "What garden was locked? Why?" Suddenly he was very interested.

"It—it was the garden Mr. Craven hates," Mary said. "He locked it. No one knows where he buried the key."

"What sort of a garden is it?" Colin asked eagerly.

"No one has been allowed in it for ten years," Mary answered carefully. But it was too late. Colin asked question after question. Where was it? Had she never looked for the door? Had she never asked the gardeners?

"I would make them tell me all about it,"declared Colin.

"Could you?" Mary began to feel even more frightened.

"I told you, everyone has to please me," he said. "If I were to live, this place would belong to me someday."

"Do you really think you won't live?" Mary asked. She was curious—but she also hoped to make him forget the garden.

"I don't suppose I shall." He sounded as though he didn't care. "People say I won't."

"Do you want to live?" inquired Mary.

"No," he answered crossly. "But I don't want to die. When I feel ill I lie here and think about it until I cry and cry."

"I have heard you crying," Mary said.

"Were you crying about that?" She did so want him to forget the garden.

"I dare say," he answered. "But let us talk about something else. Talk about that garden. I want to see it. I am going to make them take me there. And I will let you go, too."

Mary's hands clutched each other. This **horrid** boy would spoil everything! "Oh, don't...don't do that!" she cried.

He stared as if he thought she had gone crazy. "Why?" he exclaimed. "You said you wanted to see it."

"I do," she answered. "But if you make them open the door it will never be a secret again."

"A secret," Colin said. "What do you mean?"

Mary's words tumbled out. "If we could find a door, we could slip inside, and no one would know but us. And if we dug and planted seeds and made it all come alive..."

"Is it dead?" he **interrupted** her.

"It will be if no one cares for it," Mary went on. "But if we could get into it, we could help things grow. Oh, don't you see how much nicer it would be if it was a secret?"

Colin dropped back on his pillow. "I never had a secret."

"Don't make them take you," Mary pleaded. "Then we could go alone, and it would always be a secret garden."

"I should...like...that," he said very slowly.

Mary began to feel safer. Maybe, if he could see the garden in his mind, he would not want everyone **tramping** into it. "I'll tell you what I think it would be like," she said. "It has been shut up so long things have grown into a **tangle**." He lay still. Mary told him about the roses, and about the robin.

"I did not know birds could be like that," he said. "What a lot of things you know. I feel as if you had been inside that garden."

Mary did not know what to say. At last she asked, "What would Mrs. Medlock do if she found out that I had been here?"

"She would do as I told her to," he said. "And I should tell her that I wanted you to come every day. I am glad you came."

"So am I," said Mary. "I will come as often as I can. But I shall have to look every day for the garden door."

"Yes," Colin said. "Then you can tell me about it afterward." He lay still, thinking. "I think you shall be a secret, too," he said at last. "I can send the nurse out when you are here. Do you know Martha?"

"I know her very well," said Mary. "She waits on me."

"Then Martha shall tell you when to come here."

"I have been here a long time now," said Mary. "And your eyes look sleepy. Shall I go away?"

"I wish I could go to sleep before you leave me," Colin said.

"Shut your eyes," Mary said. She drew her footstool closer. "I will do what my ayah used to do. I will pat your hand and sing."

"I should like that," he said drowsily.

Mary patted his hand and sang until he was fast asleep. Then she got up softly and crept away without making a sound.

 VI. A Young Rajah

"I know what the crying was," Mary told Martha the next day. They were sitting by the fire in Mary's room.

Martha dropped her knitting. "Miss Mary!" she exclaimed. "Tha'll get me into trouble! I'll lose my place!"

"But he was nice to me," Mary said. She explained how she had found Colin. "He wants me to come see him," she finished.

Martha gasped. "I can **scarcely** believe thee. If he'd been like he is most times, he'd have thrown one of his **tantrums**."

"Is Colin a hunchback?" Mary asked. "He didn't look it."

"He isn't yet," said Martha. "But they was

afraid his back was weak so they've kept him lying down." She paused. "He's very spoiled," she added.

"I wonder if it would not do him good to go outside and watch things growing," Mary said carefully. "It did me good."

"But he hates being taken out of doors," Martha explained. "And he can't stand being looked at. One of the worst fits he ever had was when they took him out and a new gardener looked at him curious. Colin was ill all night."

"If he ever gets angry at me, I'll never go and see him again," said Mary.

"He'll have thee if he wants thee," Martha said. "Tha' may as well know that at the start."

Soon Martha was called away by the bell. When she returned, her eyes were wide with fear. "He wants thee now."

Mary went to Colin's room. "Martha is very frightened," she told him. "She is afraid Mrs. Medlock will send her away."

Colin frowned. "Go and tell her to come here," he said.

"If I order you to bring Miss Mary to me, how can Medlock send you away if she finds it out?" Colin asked Martha. "You must do as I please."

"Yes, sir. Please don't let her, sir," pleaded Martha.

"I'll send her away if she dares to say such a thing," said Colin grandly. "She wouldn't like that, I can tell you."

"Yes, sir. I want to do my duty, sir." Martha curtsied.

"What I want is your duty," said Colin, more grandly still. "I'll take care of you. Now go away."

When the door closed, Colin found Mary gazing at him. "Why do you look at me like that?" he asked her. "Sit down and tell me what you are thinking."

Mary sat on the footstool. "I was thinking two things. Once in India I saw a boy who was a **rajah**. He had jewels stuck all over him. He spoke to his people just as you spoke to Martha. Everybody had to do everything he told them, in a minute. I think they would have been killed if they hadn't."

"I shall make you tell me about rajahs presently," he said. "But first tell me what the second thing was."

"The second thing was how different you are from Dickon."

"Who is Dickon?" Colin asked.

"Dickon is Martha's brother," Mary explained. "He is not like anyone else in the world. He can charm animals."

Colin's eyes grew larger and larger. "Tell me some more about him," he said.

"He knows all animals, and everything that grows on the moor," Mary said.

"But how can he like the moor? It's such a **dreary** place!"

"But it's beautiful," protested Mary. "Thousands of lovely things grow on it. And there are so many little creatures building nests and singing or squeaking to each other."

"You never see anything if you are ill," said Colin crossly. "I could never go on the moor."

Mary was silent for a minute. "You might—sometime."

Colin looked startled. "How could I? I am going to die."

"How do you know?" said Mary boldly. She didn't like the way he talked about dying. He almost boasted about it.

"Oh, they are always whispering about it. They think I don't notice. They wish I would die, too," Colin said.

Mary frowned. "Who does?"

"The servants. And my doctor, Dr. Craven. He is my uncle. If I die, he will inherit this place. He always looks more cheerful when I am worse."

"I don't believe that," said Mary stubbornly.

Colin turned and looked at her again. "Don't you?"

"I like the grand doctor from London that you told me about," Mary said. "Did he say you were going to die?"

"No. He said, 'The lad might live if he would make up his mind to it. You must make him want to live.' But they can't."

"I'll tell you who could," said Mary. "I believe Dickon could." She pulled her stool nearer to the sofa. "See here," she said. "Let's talk about living. Let's talk about Dickon."

It was the best thing she could have said. Mary and Colin both talked as they never had before. Soon they began to laugh over nothings, as if they were two normal, happy ten-year-olds.

In the midst of the fun the door opened and in walked Dr. Craven and Mrs. Medlock. "Good Lord!" Dr. Craven exclaimed. "What is this?"

"This is my cousin, Mary," Colin said. "She heard me crying one night and found me. I am glad she came."

Dr. Craven did not look pleased. He felt Colin's pulse. "I am afraid there has been too much excitement. Excitement is not good for you, my boy," he said.

"I should be more excited if she kept away!" Colin's eyes sparkled dangerously. "I am better. She makes me better."

Dr. Craven studied Colin's face. "But you must not talk too much, my boy. You must not forget that you are ill. You must not forget that you are very easily tired."

Colin looked fretful. He kept his strange eyes fixed on Dr. Craven's face. "I want to forget it," he said at last. "She makes me forget it. That is why I want her."

 VII. "I Won't," Said Mary

There was another week of rain. Mary enjoyed herself, though there was no chance to visit the garden or Dickon. Instead, she spent hours with Colin, talking and laughing.

On the first clear, sunny morning, Mary woke very early. She dressed, then flew out the front door. When she reached the garden, she was startled to find Dickon already there. With him were a bushy-tailed fox and a large, blue-black crow.

Mary flew across the grass. "Oh, Dickon! Dickon!" she cried. "How could you get here so early?"

Dickon laughed. "Eh!" he said. "How could I have stayed in bed on a day like this! I run like mad, shouting and singing."

Neither the crow nor the fox seemed the least bit afraid of Mary. Together, they all walked round the garden. Dickon showed Mary leaf buds on rose branches that had seemed dead. He showed her ten thousand new green points pushing through the earth. They worked and laughed all morning.

Finally, they sat down on the grass to rest. Mary told Dickon how she had found Colin. She told him how Colin was always afraid there might be a lump starting on his back.

"Eh!" Dickon said. "If he was out here he'd be watching for buds to break on the rosebushes, not looking for lumps to grow on his back." He thought very hard, scratching the fox's back. "I could push his carriage well enough. It'd be good for him. Us will have him out here sometime for sure," he declared.

That afternoon, Mary returned to the house only long enough to eat her supper. "Tell Colin that I can't come yet," she said to Martha. "I must get back to the garden."

Martha looked scared. "Miss Mary, that may upset him!"

But Mary didn't care. "I can't stay," she answered. "Dickon's waiting for me."

The afternoon was even lovelier than the morning, and they worked for hours. "It'll be fine tomorrow," said Dickon when they parted. "I'll be at work by sunrise."

"So will I," Mary said. She ran all the way back to the house. She couldn't wait to tell Colin everything!

But when Mary got to Colin's room, she found him lying flat on his back in bed, not sitting up on his sofa as usual. Mary marched **stiffly** up to him. "Why didn't you get up?" she said.

"I did get up. But when you didn't come, I made them put me back in bed. My back ached and I was tired." He turned away from her. "Why didn't you come?" he **whined**.

"I was working in the garden with Dickon." Mary pinched her lips together.

Colin frowned. "I won't let that boy come here if you won't come talk to me," he said.

Mary flew into a **passion**. "If you send Dickon away, I'll never come into this room again!" she threatened.

"You'll have to if I want you," said Colin. "They shall drag you in."

"Shall they, Mr. Rajah!" said Mary fiercely. "They may drag me in, but they can't make me talk! I won't say a word!"

"Oh, you are a **selfish** thing!" cried Colin. No one had ever spoken to him like this before.

"And what are you?" said Mary. "You're the most selfish boy I ever saw."

"I'm not!" snapped Colin. "I'm not as selfish as your fine Dickon is! He keeps you playing in the dirt when he knows I am all by myself. He's selfish!"

Mary's eyes flashed fire. "Dickon is nicer than any other boy that ever lived!" she said. "He's—he's like an angel!"

"An angel! He's a common cottage boy!" Colin sneered.

"He's better than a common rajah!" retorted Mary.

Colin turned away from her. He was beginning to feel quite sorry for himself. A big tear ran down his cheek. "I'm not as selfish as you because I'm always ill. I'm sure there is a lump coming on my back," he said. "And I am going to die besides."

"You're not!" Mary shouted. "You just say that to make people feel sorry for you. I believe you're proud of it."

Colin sat up in a rage. "Get out of my room!" he shouted.

"I'm going," Mary said. "And I won't come back!" She marched to the door. "I was going to tell you all sorts of nice things," she said, turning round. "But now I won't tell you a single thing!" She turned and marched out.

Mary went back to her room feeling cross. She would never tell Colin her secret now!

But after a while her heart began to soften. She thought of the way Colin would always put a hand on his spine. That frightened Mary, because he always looked so frightened himself.

"He always thinks about it when he is cross or tired," she said to herself. "And he has been cross today. Perhaps he has been thinking about it all day..." she hesitated. "I said I would never go back again. But perhaps I will go and see...if he wants me...in the morning."

 VIII. A Tantrum

Several hours later, Mary jumped out of bed, still half-asleep. What was that awful noise?

She stood still, listening. Someone was crying and screaming. Up and down the corridor, doors opened and shut. Footsteps hurried by. "It's Colin," Mary said to herself. "He's having a tantrum." She put her hands over her ears, feeling sick and frightened. The screaming was awful. Why didn't he stop?

But suddenly Mary's fear turned to anger. She wanted to frighten Colin as he was frightening her. If no one else would stop him she would! She opened her door and flew down the corridor to his room.

The nearer she got the higher her temper

mounted. She slapped open Colin's door, running past the nurse and Mrs. Medlock. "You stop!" she shouted. "You stop! I hate you! I wish you would scream yourself to death!"

Colin was lying on his face beating the pillow. He jumped at the sound of the **furious** little voice. His face was white and red and swollen, and he was gasping and choking. But Mary did not care an **atom**. "If you scream another scream," she said, "I'll scream too! And I can scream louder than you! I'll frighten you!"

Colin actually stopped screaming, she startled him so. Tears streamed down his face. He shook all over. "I can't stop!"

"You can!" shouted Mary. "Half that **ails** you is just temper!" She stamped her foot. "Temper, temper, temper!"

"But I felt the lump—I felt it," Colin choked out. "I knew I should. I shall have a hunch on my back. And I shall die!"

"You didn't feel a lump!" Mary said fiercely. "There's nothing the matter with your horrid back! Turn over and let me see it! Nurse, show me his back this minute!" she commanded.

"Sh-show her! She-she'll see then!" Colin gasped.

The nurse did as she was told. It was a poor thin back, indeed. Mary examined it in silence, a **savage** look on her **solemn** little face. She looked up and down his spine as carefully as if she were the great doctor from London.

"There's not a single lump there!" she said at last. "There's not a lump as big as a pin, except backbone lumps. And you can only feel them because you're thin. I've got backbone lumps myself. If you ever say there is a lump again, I shall laugh!"

Colin turned on his face again. He took long, broken breaths. Great tears of relief streamed down his face. Presently he turned over again. "Do you think I could...live to grow up?" he asked **meekly**.

"You probably will if you do what you are told," the nurse said. "You must not give way to your temper. And you must stay out a great deal in the fresh air."

Colin was worn out with crying. He put out his hand toward Mary. She met him half way with her hand. "I'll—I'll go out with you, Mary," he said. "I shan't hate fresh air if we can find..." He remembered just in time to stop himself from saying, "the secret garden." He ended, "if Dickon will come and push my chair. I do so want to see Dickon and his animal friends."

After the nurse and Mrs. Medlock had left them, Colin said, "I almost told. But I stopped myself in time. I'll go to sleep, but you said you had nice things to tell me. Have you found the way into the secret garden?"

Mary looked at his poor little tired face and swollen eyes. Her heart **relented**. "Yes," she answered. "I think I have. And if you will go to sleep I will tell you about it tomorrow."

Colin's hand trembled. "Oh, Mary!" he said. "Oh, Mary! If I could get into it I think I should live to grow up! Tell me again what you think it looks like inside."

"Then shut your eyes," answered Mary. She held his hand and spoke in a low voice. "I think it has been left alone so long that it has grown into a lovely tangle. I think the roses have climbed until they hang from the walls like a strange gray mist. When the summer comes, there will be curtains and fountains of roses. I think the ground is full of **daffodils** and snow-drops and **lilies**."

The soft **drone** of her voice was making him more and more still. Mary saw it and went on. "Perhaps there are clusters of purple crocuses and gold ones even now. Perhaps the leaves are beginning to uncurl and a green **veil** is creeping over everything. And perhaps the robin has found a **mate**—and is building a nest."

And Colin was asleep.

 IX. "I Shall Get Well"

After Mary worked in the garden the next day, she was ready to tell Colin the secret. "Can I trust you for sure?" she asked him.

Her face was so solemn, Colin almost whispered. "Yes!"

Mary caught hold of his hands. "I found the door into the garden."

Colin's eyes grew bigger and bigger. "Oh! Mary!" he cried. "Shall I live to see it?" He clutched her hands and dragged her toward him.

"Of course you'll see it!" snapped Mary. Don't be silly!" That brought Colin to his senses immediately, and he began to laugh at himself.

They had to wait more than a week for the weather to be warm enough for Colin to go out. In the meantime, Dickon came to visit Colin, bringing his creatures with him--tame squirrels, the fox and the crow, and a new-born lamb. Soon Colin and Dickon were good friends.

When the day finally arrived, Colin gave strict orders. None of the gardeners were to be around when he was outside in his chair. No one was to see him.

The strongest **footman** in the house carried Colin out and settled him into his wheeled chair. Then Dickon took over, pushing the chair slowly and steadily. Mary walked beside it.

Finally they turned into the long walk. "This is it," breathed Mary.

There was a lovely **breathless** silence as the chair wheeled on.

A few yards more and Mary whispered, "This is where the robin flew over the wall. And that is where he showed me the key."

Colin sat up. "Where? Where?" he cried.

"And this is the ivy the wind blew back," Mary said. "And here is the handle, and here is the door. Dickon, push him in—quickly!" Mary said.

Colin dropped back against his cushions,

covering his eyes. When they were all inside the garden, he took his hands away and gasped. A green veil of tender leaves had crept over everything. Here and there in the grass were splashes of gold and purple and white. The trees were showing pink and white above his head. There were **flutterings** of wings, and wonderful scents.

Mary and Dickon stood and stared at Colin in wonder. He looked so strange and different. A pink glow had actually crept over him—ivory face and neck and hands and all.

"I shall get well! I shall get well!" he cried out.

They drew Colin's chair under the plum tree, which was snow-white with blossoms. Mary and Dickon worked for hours as Colin watched. "I don't want this afternoon to go," Colin said. "But I shall come back tomorrow, and the day after, and the day after."

"That tha' will," said Dickon. "Us will have thee walking about here and digging same as other folk before long."

Colin **flushed**. "Walk!" he said. "Dig! Shall I?"

"For sure tha' will," Dickon said. "Tha's got

legs, same as other folks!"

"Nothing really ails them," Colin said. "But they are so thin and weak I'm afraid to try to stand on them."

"When tha' stops being afraid, tha' shall stand on them," Dickon said.

Colin lay still for a long while, thinking. Then, suddenly, he pointed at the far garden wall. "Who is that man?" he exclaimed.

Mary and Dickon wheeled about. Ben Weatherstaff was standing on a ladder, glaring at them over the wall. He shook his fist at Mary. "Tha' bad young thing!" he cried, "Always poking tha' nose where it was not wanted!"

Suddenly Ben stopped shaking his fist. He stared at something behind her. A wheeled chair had come toward him, a young rajah in it.

Colin held out a thin white hand to Ben. "Do you know who I am?" he demanded.

"Who tha' art?" Ben said. His voice shook. "Aye, tha' art the poor **cripple**."

Colin flushed **scarlet**. "I'm not a cripple!"

"He's not!" cried Mary, almost shouting. "He's not got a lump as big as a pin! I looked and there was none—not one!"

Ben stared. "Tha' hasn't got a crooked back and crooked legs?"

"No!" shouted Colin. He had never been accused of crooked legs before! Dickon rushed to his side. There was a fierce scramble. The blankets were tossed aside. Dickon held Colin's arm.

The thin legs were out, the thin feet on the grass. Colin stood, as straight as an arrow. "Look at me!" he cried. "Just look at me, you!"

Ben gulped. Suddenly tears ran down his weather-wrinkled cheeks. "Eh, the lies folk tells!" he burst forth. "There's not a **knob** on thee."

Colin looked Ben Weatherstaff in the face. "I'm your master when my father is away," he said. "Go out to the long walk and Mary will bring you here. I want to talk to you!"

"Yes, sir," Ben said.

Colin leaned against a tree so his legs would not give way. "Look at me!" he commanded when Ben came through the door. "Am I a hunchback? Have I got crooked legs?"

"Not tha'," Ben said.

"Everyone thought I was going to die," said Colin shortly. "But I'm not!"

Colin sat down. "This is my garden now,"

he told Ben. "I shall send for you to help some-times. But it is to be a secret."

"Aye, sir," answered Ben.

Colin picked up a **trowel** that Mary had dropped. He began to scratch at the earth. His hand was weak. Still, he drove the trowel into the soil and began to dig.

"You can do it!" said Mary to herself.

Ben looked on. "How would tha' like to plant something?" he asked. "I can get thee a rose in a pot."

"Yes, get it!" said Colin, digging excitedly.

Dickon helped dig the hole. Ben brought the rose from the greenhouse.

Flushed and glowing, Colin looked up at the sky. "I want to do it before the sun goes down," he said.

"Here, lad," Ben said, handing the plant to Colin. "Set it in the earth."

Colin's thin white hands shook a little. He filled in the earth and pressed it down.

"It's planted!" said Colin. "Help me up, Dickon. I want to be standing when the sun goes down." And Dickon did, so when the sun set, Colin stood on his two feet—laughing.

 X. Magic

In the months that followed, it seemed as if there truly was Magic in the secret garden. Mary's seeds grew as if fairies **tended** them. And the roses...the roses! Rising out of the grass, tangled round the sundial, **wreathing** the tree trunks...they came alive day by day.

Colin spent every day in the garden, watching things grow. He became fascinated by Magic, and talked of it **constantly**. Then one day he made an announcement: "When I grow up I am going to make great **scientific discoveries**. These discoveries will be about Magic. I am sure there is Magic in everything, but we have not sense enough to make it do things."

"The Magic in this garden has made me

stand," he went on. "Now I know I am going to live to be a man. I am going to make the scientific **experiment** of trying to put some Magic in myself. And you must all do it, too."

Colin began to chant, "The Magic is in me! It's in us all! Magic! Come and help!"

Colin said this many times. "Now I am going to walk round the garden," he announced. He leaned on Dickon's arm, with Mary on his other side and Ben behind them.

They moved slowly but with **dignity**. Now and then Colin walked a few steps alone. He held his head high. It seemed certain that something was uplifting him.

He returned to where they had begun, looking **triumphant**. "The Magic worked!" he cried. "That is my first discovery!"

"What will Dr. Craven say?" Mary asked.

"He won't say anything," Colin answered. "He will not be told. I shall come here every day in my chair and I shall be taken back in it. My father won't hear about it until he comes back to Misselthwaite. I shall walk into his study and say "Here I am. I am well. It has been done by a scientific experiment."

One day the nurse said to Colin, "Your **appetite** is improving. You used to eat so little, and so much **disagreed** with you."

"Nothing disagrees with me now," Colin said. Suddenly he remembered that he shouldn't seem too well just yet. "At least things don't so often disagree with me. It's the fresh air."

"Perhaps. But I must talk to Dr. Craven," the nurse said.

When Dr. Craven came he seemed puzzled, too. "You stay out in the garden a great deal. I suppose it has done you no harm. The nurse says your appetite is quite good."

"Perhaps," said Colin. Suddenly he felt inspired. "But perhaps it is an **unnatural** appetite. Perhaps I am **bloated** and **feverish**," he added gloomily. "People who are not going to live are so often...different."

Dr. Craven shook his head. He pushed up Colin's sleeve and felt his arm. "You are not feverish. And the weight you have gained is healthy. Your father will be happy about this."

Colin sat up in alarm. "I won't have him told!" he said fiercely. "It will only disappoint him if I get worse again!"

"Hush, my boy," said Dr. Craven. "Nothing shall be written without your **permission**."

Then one morning Dickon brought two pails his mother had prepared after Dickon had told her of the children's secret. One was full of rich milk and the other held **currant** buns folded in a clean napkin. Colin and Mary were delighted.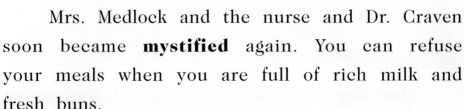

Mrs. Medlock and the nurse and Dr. Craven soon became **mystified** again. You can refuse your meals when you are full of rich milk and fresh buns.

"They eat next to nothing," said the nurse. "And yet see how they look."

"Well, so long as not eating agrees with them we need not worry," Dr. Craven said. "The boy is a new creature."

"So is the girl," said Mrs. Medlock. "She used to be such an **ill-natured** little thing! Now the two of them laugh together like crazy young ones. Perhaps they're growing fat on that."

"Perhaps they are," said Dr. Craven. "Let them laugh."

 ## XI. In the Garden

One day, after several weeks of working in the garden, Colin made a discovery. He stretched himself to his tallest height and threw out his arms. His strange eyes widened with joy. "Mary! Dickon!" he cried. "Just look at me! I'm well–I'm truly well!" Colin declared.

"Aye, that tha' art!" said Dickon.

"I'm well! I'm well!" said Colin again, and his face went red all over. He had known it before in a way. But at that minute something had rushed through him. It was a belief so strong he could not help calling out. "I shall live forever and ever," he cried grandly. "And I shall never stop making Magic!"

That same day, Dickon's mother came to

visit the children. She saw how well he looked, and knew how much he wished that his father would return home to see how he had changed. The children would not be able to fool the doctor and Mrs. Medlock much longer, it was clear. Mrs. Sowerby decided she must do something to help.

While the secret garden was coming alive, Archibald Craven was wandering about beautiful places in Europe. For ten long years he had let his **soul** fill itself with blackness.

Then one day a strange thing happened. He had been walking through a wonderful valley in **Austria**. At last he felt tired. He sat down to rest by a stream, and his mind grew quiet.

Mr. Craven found himself looking at a mass of **forget-me-nots** at the water's edge, thinking how lovely it was. That simple thought seemed to push aside the blackness in his mind.

At last he got up slowly and drew a deep breath. Something had changed inside him. "I almost feel as if I were alive!" he whispered. (Later, he found out that on this day Colin had cried out: "I am going to live forever and ever!")

From that day on, Mr. Craven began to wonder if he should not go home. Now and then he thought about his boy. Like the garden, he was slowly "coming alive."

The next morning, Mr. Craven received a letter from Dickon's mother. He opened it and read, "Dear Sir: I would come home if I was you. I think you would be glad to come and—if you will excuse me, sir—I think your lady would ask you to come if she was here. Your servant, Susan Sowerby."

Mr. Craven read the letter twice, thinking about the dream. "I will go back to Misselthwaite at once," he decided.

On his long trip home he found himself thinking of his boy. He had not meant to be a bad father, but he had not felt like a father at all. When he had seen the child's great gray eyes—so like his wife's, and yet so unlike them—he had not been able to stand it. He had turned away, pale as death. After that he hardly ever saw the boy except when Colin was asleep.

All this was not a happy thing to recall. But as the train drew closer to Misselthwaite, Mr. Craven began to think in a new way. Was it possible that Mrs. Sowerby thought he could do the boy good? Was that why she had written?

When he arrived at the manor he went into the library. He sent for Mrs. Medlock. "How is Master Colin?" he asked.

Mrs. Medlock flushed. "To tell the truth, sir, Master Colin might be better. Or he might be changing for the worse." She told Mr. Craven about Colin's strange eating habits, and how he insisted on going out every day.

"Where is he now?" Mr. Craven asked.

"In the garden, sir. He's always in the garden."

"In the garden," Mr. Craven repeated. He left the house and turned into the long walk. Mrs. Medlock could not have meant that garden—yet he felt drawn to it.

His step slowed. He knew where the door was under the ivy. But he did not know where the buried key lay. So he stopped, and stood looking about.

Soon he started. No one had passed through the garden door for ten lonely years. And yet, inside were the sounds of **scuffling** feet and **smothered** cries! It sounded like children trying not to be heard! Was he mad?

Then the sounds forgot to hush themselves.

The feet ran faster and faster. There was a wild **outbreak** of laughter, and the door in the wall was flung open. The ivy swung back, and a boy burst through it. He dashed almost into Mr. Craven's arms.

Mr. Craven reached out just in time to save himself from falling. He held the boy away to look at him. He was tall and handsome, full of life.

Then the boy lifted a pair of strange gray eyes to the man's face. Mr. Craven gasped. "Who...what?" he stammered.

This was not what Colin had planned. And yet to come dashing out—winning a race—perhaps it was even better. He drew himself up to his very tallest. "Father," he said, "I'm Colin. You can't believe it. I scarcely can myself. I'm Colin."

"It was the garden that did it," said Colin. "And Mary and Dickon. And the Magic. We kept it secret until you came. I'm well!" Colin put his hand on his father's arm. "Aren't you glad, Father? I'm going to live forever and ever!"

Mr. Craven's soul shook with joy. He put his hands on the boy's shoulders. He did not dare to speak at first. "Take me into the garden," he said at last. "And tell me all about it."

And so they led him in. The place was a **wilderness** of autumn gold and purple and flaming scarlet. Late roses climbed and hung everywhere. They sat down under their tree—all but Colin. He wanted to stand while he told the story.

Archibald Craven thought it was the strangest thing he had ever heard. He laughed until tears came into his eyes.

"Now," Colin said at the end of the story, "it need not be a secret any more. I dare say it will frighten the servants when they see me. But I am never going to get into that chair again."

And so it was that the servants of Misselthwaite beheld an amazing sight that day. Soon the master returned to the house. And by his side, with his head high and his eyes full of laughter, walked as strongly and steadily as any boy in Yorkshire—Master Colin.

# GLOSSARY

ails

appetite

art

atom

Austria

Ayah

aye

beggar

bleak

bloated

breathless

brood

buried

carriage

charm

cheeky

chirp

cholera

clod

constantly

corridor

courting

cripple

crocuses

crossly

currant

daffodils

daffy-down-dillys

delicate

dignity

disagreed

discoveries

dreary

drone

enchanting

epidemic

exclaimed

experiment

| | |
|---|---|
| feverish | manor |
| fledgling | mate |
| flushed | meekly |
| flutterings | midday |
| footman | miserable |
| footstool | missel thrush |
| forget-me-nots | Misselthwaite |
| fretful | moor |
| fretfully | mysterious |
| furious | mystified |
| horrid | obviously |
| housemaid | odder |
| hunchback | outbreak |
| ill-natured | passion |
| India | permission |
| indignantly | rajah |
| interrupted | relented |
| knob | robin redbreast |
| lad | rose-trees |
| lilies | savage |
| London | scarcely |

| | |
|---|---|
| scarlet | tendrils |
| scientific | tha' |
| scuffling | thee |
| selfish | thy |
| smothered | torrents |
| snowdrops | tramping |
| solemn | treetops |
| soul | triumphant |
| sour | trowel |
| spade | unnatural |
| stammered | veil |
| stiffly | voyage |
| stolen | wench |
| stoutly | whined |
| surly | wilderness |
| tangle | wintry |
| tantrums | wreathing |
| tapestries | Yorkshire |
| tended | |